Nursery rhymes are themselves: they are basic. They have here returned to base. In our modern world they appear in many forms. Those that are meant for the home but that add elaborate displays in the accompaniment serve only to show up how resistant are these tough, enduring little entities of his own folklore that are every child's heritage, to attempts upon their real nature. These offered here belong where they begin, on mother's knee, and find unadorned their simplest essential.

Because for the intimacy of shared performance, nursery rhymes lend themselves most faithfully to accompaniment upon a keyboard instrument, and a piano is in many homes, these accompaniments are devised for any parent of little musical skill and a child upon his lap. To this extent it is a musician's book, of one who first knew rhymes in this way and has gone on loving them so long as life is.

It is not sufficiently realized that as the tunes are meant for singing, there are many which it is inappropriate necessarily to try and reproduce upon an instrument. They simply need underpinning. Once the tune is known and sung, hand positions established, piano fingers move by easy step, no more demanded than to keep things going.

This collection is founded on the rhymes included in those gracious classics *The Baby's Opera* and *The Baby's Bouquet* and their antecedents, the rhymes and tunes edited and the accompaniments brought up to date in our own time. May it bring all who grow from these roots to the joyful truth "in my end is my beginning."

ELIZABETH POSTON

THE BABY'S SONG BOOK

ELIZABETH POSTON

WITH ILLUSTRATIONS BY
WILLIAM STOBBS

THOMAS Y. CROWELL COMPANY
NEW YORK

because of
Clementine

———

for dear Elizabeth Craggs

———

Philip and
Anthea

CONTENTS

THE BABY'S SONG BOOK

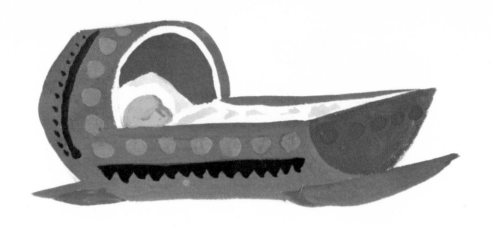

BYE, BABY BUNTING

Bye, ba - by bunt - ing, Dad - dy's gone a - hunt - ing,

Gone to get a rab - bit skin To wrap the ba - by

bunt - ing in. Bye, ba - by bunt - ing.

Bye, baby bunting,
Daddy's gone a-hunting,
Gone to get a rabbit skin
To wrap the baby bunting in.
Bye, baby bunting.

THREE CHILDREN SLIDING
ON THE ICE

1 Three chil-dren slid-ing on the ice Up-on a sum-mer's day, ____ It so fell out, they all fell in, The rest ____ they ran a-way. ____

1 Three children sliding on the ice
      Upon a summer's day,
   It so fell out, they all fell in,
      The rest they ran away.

2 Now had these children been at home,
      Or sliding on dry ground,
   Ten thousand pounds to one penny
      They had not all been drown'd.

3 You parents all that children have,
      And you that have got none,
   If you would keep them safe abroad,
      Pray keep them safe at home.

DANCE A BABY, DIDDY

Dance a ba - by, did - dy, ____

What can mam-my do wid 'e, ____ But sit in her lap, And

give 'un some pap, And dance a ba - by did-dy?

Dance a baby, diddy,
What can mammy do wid 'e,
But sit in her lap,
And give 'un some pap,
And dance a baby diddy?

FIDDLE-DE-DEE

Fid - dle - de - dee, Fid - dle - de - dee, The

fly has mar - ried the hum - ble - bee.

Fine

1 Says the fly, says he, Will you mar - ry me, And

live with me, Sweet hum - ble - bee?

Fiddle-de-dee, Fiddle-de-dee,
The fly has married the humble-bee. (*twice*)

1   Says the fly, says he,
     Will you marry me,
  And live with me,
     Sweet humble-bee?
     Fiddle-de-dee, &c.

2   Says the bee, says she,
     I'll live under your wing,
  And you'll never know
     That I carry a sting.
     Fiddle-de-dee, &c.

3   So when the parson
     Had joined the pair,
  They both went out
     To take the air.
     Fiddle-de-dee, &c.

4   And the fly did buzz
     And the bells did ring
  Did you ever hear
     So merry a thing?
     Fiddle-de-dee, &c.

5   And then to think
     That of all the flies
  The humble-bee
     Should carry the prize.
     Fiddle-de-dee, &c.

YANKEE DOODLE

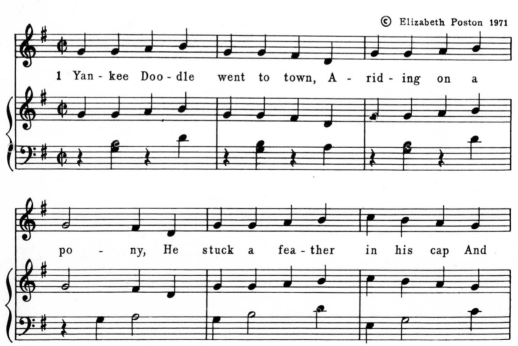

1 Yan-kee Doo-dle went to town, A - rid-ing on a

po - ny, He stuck a fea-ther in his cap And

called it Ma-ca-ro-ni. Yan-kee Doo-dle, keep it up, Yan-kee Doo-dle Dan-dy, Mind the mu-sic and the step, And with the girls be han-dy.

1 Yankee Doodle went to town,
   A-riding on a pony,
   He stuck a feather in his cap
   And called it Macaroni.
   Yankee Doodle, keep it up,
   Yankee Doodle Dandy,
   Mind the music and the step,
   And with the girls be handy.

2 Father and I went down to camp,
   Along with Captain Gooding,
   And there we saw the men and boys
   As thick as hasty pudding.
   Yankee Doodle, &c.

3 There was Captain Washington
   Upon a slapping stallion,
   A-giving orders to his men,
   I guess it was a million.
   Yankee Doodle, &c.

4 I can't tell you half I see,
   They kept up such a smother,
   So I took my hat off, made a bow,
   And scampered home to mother.
   Yankee Doodle, &c.

THE FOUR BROTHERS

1 I had four bro - thers o - ver the sea,

Per - rie Mer - rie Dix - i Do - mi - ne; And they

each sent a pre - sent un - to me. Pe - trum, Par - trum,

Pa-ra-di-si Tem-po-re, Per-rie Mer-rie Dix - i Do - mi - ne.

1 I had four brothers over the sea,
       Perrie Merrie Dixi Domine;
   And they each sent a present unto me.
       Petrum, Partrum, Paradisi Tempore,
       Perrie Merrie Dixi Domine.

2 The first sent a goose without a bone,
       Perrie Merrie Dixi Domine;
   The second sent a cherry without a stone,
       Petrum, Partrum, Paradisi Tempore,
       Perrie Merrie Dixi Domine.

3 The third sent a blanket without a thread,
       Perrie Merrie Dixi Domine;
   The fourth sent a book that no man could read.
       Petrum, Partrum, Paradisi Tempore,
       Perrie Merrie Dixi Domine.

4 When the cherry's in the blossom, there is no stone,
       Perrie Merrie Dixi Domine;
   When the goose is in the egg-shell, there is no bone,
       Petrum, Partrum, Paradisi Tempore,
       Perrie Merrie Dixi Domine.

5 When the wool's on the sheep's back there's no thread,
       Perrie Merrie Dixi Domine;
   When the book's in the press, no man it can read.
       Petrum, Partrum, Paradisi Tempore,
       Perrie Merrie Dixi Domine.

SING A SONG OF SIXPENCE

1 Sing a song of six – pence, A poc – ket – ful of rye;

Four and twen – ty black – birds Baked in a pie;

When the pie was o – pened, The birds be – gan to sing;

Was-n't that a dain-ty dish To set be-fore the king?

1 Sing a song of sixpence,
   A pocketful of rye;
   Four and twenty blackbirds
   Baked in a pie;
   When the pie was opened,
   The birds began to sing;
   Wasn't that a dainty dish
   To set before the king?

2 The king was in his counting-house,
   Counting out his money;
   The queen was in the parlour,
   Eating bread and honey;
   The maid was in the garden,
   Hanging out the clothes,
   When up came a blackbird,
   And snapped off her nose.

PUSSY CAT HIGH,
PUSSY CAT LOW

1 Pus - sy cat high,   Pus - sy cat low,

Pus - sy cat was a fine tea - ser of tow.

1   Pussy cat high, Pussy cat low,
    Pussy cat was a fine teaser of tow.

2   Pussy cat she came into the barn,
    With her bagpipes under her arm.

3   And then she told a tale to me,
    How Mousey had married a humble-bee.

4   Then was I ever so glad
    That Mousey had married so clever a lad.

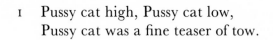

HOTTE, HOTTE REITERPFERD

GEE-UP, GEE-UP LITTLE HORSE
(KNEE-RIDE)

Hot - te, hot - te Rei - ter - pferd, das Pferd ist nicht drei
Gee - up, gee - up lit - tle horse, You don't cost a

Hel - ler werth. Wenn die Kin - der klei - ne sind,
pen - ny - worth. While the chil - dren still are small,

reit'n sie auf dem Steck - en rum; Wenn sie grös - ser
Hob - by - horse is best of all; When they're big and

wer - den, reit'n sie auf den Pfer - den; Geht das Pferd - chen
bon - ny, A horse they'll ride, or po - ny; Trit trit trot, We're

tripp tripp trapp! fall'n die Kin - der al - le 'rab.
off to town; One, two, three, You all fall down.

Hotte, hotte Reiterpferd,
das Pferd ist nicht drei Heller werth.
Wenn die Kinder kleine sind,
reit'n sie auf dem Stecken rum;
Wenn sie grösser werden,
reit'n sie auf den Pferden;
    Geht das Pferdchen
    tripp tripp trapp!
    fall'n die Kinder
    alle 'rab.

Gee-up, gee-up little horse,
You don't cost a pennyworth.
While the children still are small,
Hobby-horse is best of all;
When they're big and bonny,
A horse they'll ride, or pony;
    Trit trit trot!
    We're off to town;
    One, two, three,
    You all fall down.

LITTLE BOY BLUE

Lit - tle Boy Blue, Come blow up your horn, The

sheep's in the mea - dow, The cow's in the corn. But

where is the boy Who looks af - ter the sheep? He's

un - der a hay - cock, Fast a - sleep. Will__ you wake him?

No, not I; For if__ I do, He's sure to cry.

Little Boy Blue,
  Come blow up your horn,
The sheep's in the meadow,
  The cow's in the corn.
But where is the boy
  Who looks after the sheep?
He's under a hay-cock,
  Fast asleep.
Will you wake him?
  No, not I;
For if I do,
  He's sure to cry.

A FROG HE WOULD
A-WOOING GO

© Elizabeth Poston 1971

1 A frog he would a-woo - ing go, Heigh - ho! says Row - ley, ___ A frog he would a-woo - ing go, ___ Whe-ther his mo-ther would let him or no. With a row - ley, pow - ley,

gam-mon and spi-nach, Heigh - ho! says An-tho-ny Row-ley.

1 A frog he would a-wooing go,
    Heigh-ho! says Rowley,
A frog he would a-wooing go,
Whether his mother would let him or no.
    With a rowley, powley, gammon and spinach,
    Heigh-ho! says Anthony Rowley.

2 Pray, Mister Rat, will you go with me?
    Heigh-ho! says Rowley,
Pray, Mister Rat, will you go with me,
Kind Mrs Mousey for to see?
    With a rowley, powley, &c.

3 Pray, Mrs Mouse, are you within?
    Heigh-ho! says Rowley,
Pray, Mrs Mouse, are you within?
O yes, kind sirs, I'm sitting to spin.
    With a rowley, powley, &c.

4 Then out there came the dusty mouse,
    Heigh-ho! says Rowley,
Then out there came the dusty mouse:
I am the lady of this house.
    With a rowley, powley, &c.

5 O hast thou any mind of me?
    Heigh-ho! says Rowley,
O hast thou any mind of me?
O yes, I have great mind of thee.
    With a rowley, powley, &c.

6 Who shall this marriage make?
    Heigh-ho! says Rowley,
Who shall this marriage make?
Our lord the rat, he shall it make.
    With a rowley, powley, &c.

7 What shall we have to supper?
    Heigh-ho! says Rowley,
What shall we have to supper?
Three beans in a pound of butter.
    With a rowley, powley, &c.

8 But while they all were merry-making,
    Heigh-ho! says Rowley,
But while they all were merry-making,
A cat and her kittens came tumbling in.
    With a rowley, powley, &c.

9 The cat she seized the rat by the crown,
    Heigh-ho! says Rowley,
The cat she seized the rat by the crown,
The kittens they pulled the little mouse down.
    With a rowley, powley, &c.

10 This put Mr Frog in a terrible fright,
    Heigh-ho! says Rowley,
This put Mr Frog in a terrible fright,
He took up his hat and he wished them
    With a rowley, powley, &c.   [good night.

11 But as Froggy was crossing over the brook,
    Heigh-ho! says Rowley,
But as Froggy was crossing over the brook,
Then Dick our drake came and gobbled him up.
    With a rowley, powley, &c.

12 So there was an end of one, two, three,
    Heigh-ho! says Rowley,
So there was an end of one, two, three,
The rat, the mouse, and the little frog-ee.
    With a rowley, powley, &c.

OVER THE HILLS
AND FAR AWAY

© Elizabeth Poston 1971

1 Tom he _ was_ a_ pi-per's son, He learnt to_ play when

he was young, And all_ the_ tune_ that_ he could play Was,

'O - ver the hills and_ far a - way'. O - ver the hills and a

great way off, The wind shall blow my top-knot off.

1   Tom he was a piper's son,
He learnt to play when he was young,
And all the tune that he could play
Was, 'Over the hills and far away'.
Over the hills and a great way off,
The wind shall blow my top-knot off.

2   Tom with his pipe made such a noise,
That he pleased both girls and boys,
And they all stopped to hear him play
'Over the hills and far away'.
Over the hills and a great way off,
The wind shall blow my top-knot off.

NUTS IN MAY

1 Here we come gath - er - ing nuts in May, nuts in May, nuts in May, Here we come gath-er - ing nuts in May *On a cold and frost - y morn - ing.*

1 Here we come gathering nuts in May,
   nuts in May, nuts in May,
Here we come gathering nuts in May
On a cold and frosty morning.

2 Who shall we have for nuts in May,
   nuts in May, nuts in May?
Who shall we have for nuts in May?
On a cold and frosty morning.

3 We'll have . . . for nuts in May,

4 Who shall we send to fetch him away?
   her

5 We'll send . . . to fetch him away,
   her
Repeat verses 1–5

6 Here we come gathering nuts in May,

AU CLAIR DE LA LUNE

BY THE LIGHT OF MOONSHINE

Au clair de la lu - ne, Mon a - mi Pier - rot,
By the light of moon - shine, My good friend Pier - rot,

Prê - te-moi ta plu - me Pour é - crire un mot.
Lend to me your pen, So I may write a note.

Ma chan-delle est mor - te, Je n'ai plus de feu;
See, my can-dle's gut - tered, Dim and chill my way;

Prê - te - moi ta plu - me Pour l'a - mour de Dieu.
Lend it to me, for the Love of God, I pray.

Au clair de la lune,
   Mon ami Pierrot,
Prête-moi ta plume
   Pour écrire un mot.
Ma chandelle est morte,
   Je n'ai plus de feu ;
Prête-moi ta plume
   Pour l'amour de Dieu.

By the light of moonshine,
   My good friend Pierrot,
Lend to me your pen,
   So I may write a note.
See, my candle's guttered,
   Dim and chill my way;
Lend it to me, for the
   Love of God, I pray.

LOOBY LOO

1 Here we come loo-by loo, Here we come loo-by light,

Here we come loo-by loo-by,— All on a Sat-ur-day night.

Put your right/left hand in,— And put your right/left hand out,—

Shake it a lit-tle, a lit-tle, a lit-tle, And

turn your-self a - bout.___ Loo - by, loo - by,

D.C.

loo - by, loo - by, Loo - by, loo - by light.___

1   Here we come looby loo,
    Here we come looby light,
    Here we come looby looby,
       All on a Saturday night.

    Put your right/left hand in,

    And put your right/left hand out,

    Shake it a little, a little, a little,
       And turn yourself about.
       Looby, looby, looby, looby,
       Looby, looby light.

2   Here we come &c.
       All on a Saturday night.

    Put your right/left foot in,

    And put your right/left foot out,

    Shake it a little, a little, a little,
       And turn yourself about.
       Looby, looby, &c.

    Here we come looby loo,
    Here we come looby light,
    Here we come looby looby,
       All on a Saturday night.

MY FATHER IS DEAD

1 My fa-ther is dead, but I can't_ tell you how, He left me six hor-ses to fol-low the plough: *With my whim, wham, wad-dle O, Jack sing sad-dle O,*

1 My father is dead, but I can't tell you how,
   He left me six horses to follow the plough:
       With my whim, wham, waddle O,
       Jack sing saddle O,
       Blowsey boys, bubble O,
       Over the brow.

2 I sold my six horses and bought me a cow;
   I'd fain have made a fortune, but didn't know how:
       With my whim, wham, &c.

3 I sold my cow and I bought me a calf;
   I never made a bargain but I lost the better half:
       With my whim, wham, &c.

4 I sold my calf and I bought me a cat,
   To lie down by the fire and warm its little back:
       With my whim, wham, &c.

5 I sold my cat and I bought me a mouse,
   But she took fire in her tail, and burnt down my house:
       With my whim, wham, &c.

I LOVE SIXPENCE

1 I love six - pence, jol - ly lit - tle six - pence,

I love six - pence bet - ter than my life;

I spent a pen - ny of it, I lent a pen - ny of it,

46

And I took four-pence home to my wife.

1   I love sixpence, jolly little sixpence,
    I love sixpence better than my life;
  I spent a penny of it, I lent a penny of it,
    And I took fourpence home to my wife.

2   I love fourpence, jolly little fourpence,
    I love fourpence better than my life;
  I spent a penny of it, I lent a penny of it,
    And I took twopence home to my wife.

3   I love twopence, jolly little twopence,
    I love twopence better than my life;
  I spent a penny of it, I lent a penny of it,
    And I took nothing home to my wife.

4   I love nothing, jolly little nothing,
    What will nothing buy for my wife?
  I have nothing, I spend nothing,
    I love nothing better than my wife.

GIRA, GIRA TONDO

RING-A-RING-A ROUND-O

Gi - ra, gi - ra ton - do, Il pa - ne sot-to il for - no, Un

Ring - a - ring - a round - O, The bread is bak-ing brown - O, A

maz - zo di vi - o - le, Le do - no a chi le vuo - le; Le

bunch of vio-lets, pick them To give to the one who wants them; We'll

vuo - le la San-dri - na, E cas-chi la più pic - ci - na.
give them to the tall - est, And down falls the one that's small - est.

Gira, gira tondo,
Il pane sotto il forno,
Un mazzo di viole,
Le dono a chi le vuole;
Le vuole la Sandrina,
E caschi la più piccina.

Ring-a-ring-a round-O,
The bread is baking brown-O,
A bunch of violets, pick them
To give to the one who wants them;
We'll give them to the tallest,
And down falls the one that's smallest.

HICKETY, PICKETY, MY BLACK HEN

© Elizabeth Poston 1971
Words and tune coll. E.P.

Hick - e - ty, pick - e - ty, my black hen,

She lays eggs for gen - tle - men; Gen - tle - men come

ev - 'ry day To see what my black hen doth lay.

Hickety, pickety, my black hen,
She lays eggs for gentlemen;
Gentlemen come every day
To see what my black hen doth lay.

MARY, MARY,
QUITE CONTRARY

Ma - ry, Ma - ry, quite con - tra - ry,

How does your gar - den grow?____ With sil - ver bells and

cock - le shells, And pret - ty maids all in a row.

Mary, Mary, quite contrary,
How does your garden grow?
With silver bells and cockle shells,
And pretty maids all in a row.

DONDE ESTAN LAS LLAVES?

WHERE ARE THE KEYS OF THE CASTLE?

1 Yo ten - go un cas - til - lo, ma - ta -
1 I've a fine big cas - tle, ma - ta -

ri - le - ri - le - ri - le, Yo ten - go un cas -
ril - lay - ril - lay - ril - lay, I've a fine big

til - lo, ma - ta - ri - le - ri - le - ron, pin - pón.
cas - tle, ma - ta - ril - lay - ril - lay - ron, pim - pom.

1 Yo tengo un castillo,
     matarile-rile-rile,
   Yo tengo un castillo,
     matarile-rile-ron,
       pin-pón.

2 ¿Dónde están las llaves?

3 En el fondo del mar,

4 ¿Quién irá a buscarlas?

5 Irá Carmencita,

6 ¿Qué oficio le pondrá?

7 Le pondremos peinadora,

8 Este oficio tiene multa,

1 I've a fine big castle,
     matarillay-rillay-rillay,
   I've a fine big castle,
     matarillay-rillay-ron,
       pim-pom.

2 Where're the keys of the castle?

3 On the deep sea bottom,

4 Who will go and fetch them?

5 We'll send . . . to fetch them,

6 What's the trade we'll give her?
                                 him?

7 We'll make her him a hairdresser,

8 That trade pays a forfeit,

GIRLS AND BOYS COME OUT TO PLAY

© Elizabeth Poston 1971

Girls and boys come out to play, The
Leave your sup - per and leave your sleep, And

moon doth shine as bright as day.
come to your play - fel - lows in the street.

Come with a whoop and

come with a call, Come with a good will or not at all.

Up the lad-der and down the wall, A half-penny loaf___ will serve us all; You find milk, and I'll find flour, And

2nd time
D.C.

we'll have a pud-ding in half an hour.

Girls and boys come out to play,
The moon doth shine as bright as day.
Leave your supper and leave your sleep,
And come to your playfellows in the street.
Come with a whoop and come with a call,
Come with a good will or not at all.
Up the ladder and down the wall,
A halfpenny loaf will serve us all;
You find milk, and I'll find flour,
And we'll have a pudding in half an hour.

A SHIP A-SAILING

1 A ship, a ship a-sail - ing, A - sail - ing on the

sea, And it was deep - ly la - den With

1 A ship, a ship a-sailing,
    A-sailing on the sea,
And it was deeply laden
    With pretty things for me;
There were raisins in the cabin,
    And almonds in the hold;
The sails were made of satin,
    And the mast it was of gold.

2 The four-and-twenty sailors
    That stood between the decks,
Were four-and-twenty white mice
    With rings about their necks;
The captain was a duck, a duck,
    With a jacket on his back,
And when this fairy ship set sail,
    The captain he said Quack!

LITTLE BO-PEEP

1 Little Bo-Peep, she lost her sheep, And can't tell where to find them; Leave them alone, and they'll come home, And bring their tails behind them.

1 Little Bo-Peep, she lost her sheep,
    And can't tell where to find them;
Leave them alone, and they'll come home,
    And bring their tails behind them.

2 Little Bo-Peep fell fast asleep,
    And dreamt she heard them bleating;
But when she awoke, she found it a joke,
    For they were still a-fleeting.

3 Then up she took her little crook,
    Determined for to find them;
She found them indeed, but it made her heart bleed,
    For they'd left their tails behind them.

4 It happened one day, as Bo-Peep did stray
    Into a meadow hard by,
There she espied their tails side by side,
    All hung on a tree to dry.

5 She heaved a sigh, and wiped her eye,
    And over the hillocks went rambling,
And tried what she could, as a shepherdess should,
    To tack again each to its lambkin.

ARROYO CLARO
CLEAR-RUNNING STREAM

1 A - rro - yo cla - ro, fuen - te se - re - na, quién
1 O clear - run-ning stream, O foun - tain se - rene, who

te la-va el pa - ñue - lo sa - ber qui - sie - ra.
wash - es out your ker - chief, O who makes it clean?

1	Arroyo claro,	1	O clear-running stream,
	fuente serena,		O fountain serene,
	quién te lava el pañuelo		who washes out your kerchief,
	saber quisiera.		O who makes it clean?
2	Me lo han lavado,	2	It's washed there for me,
	me lo han tendido		was put down to dry
	en el romero verde		upon the flower that's bloomed
	que ha florecido.		on the green rosemary.
3	Arroyo claro,	3	O clear-running stream,
	fuente serena,		O fountain serene,
	quién te lava el pañuelo		who washes out your kerchief,
	saber quisiera.		O who makes it clean?
4	Me lo ha lavado	4	'Twas washed there for me
	una serrana		by a mountaineer
	en el río de Atocha		in the river of Atocha
	que corre el agua.		whose water runs clear.
5	Una lo lava,	5	And one washes it;
	otra lo tiende,		and one makes it dry,
	otra le tira rosas		one throws on it carnations,
	y otra, claveles.		one roses, to lie.
6	¡Tú eres la rosa;	6	It's you are the rose,
	yo, soy el lirio,		the lily am I,
	quién fuera cordón de oro		who'd be the golden cord
	de tu justillo!		that your garment's laced by!

THE OLD MAN
CLOTHED IN LEATHER

One mist-y moist-y morn-ing, When cloud-y was the wea-ther, There I met an old man Clothed all in lea-ther; Clothed all in lea-ther, With cap un-der his chin, With How d'you do, and

how d'you do, And How d'you do — a - gain, a - gain?

One misty moisty morning,
When cloudy was the weather,
There I met an old man
Clothed all in leather;
Clothed all in leather,
With cap under his chin,
With How d'you do, and how d'you do,
And How d'you do again, again?

HERE WE GO ROUND
THE MULBERRY BUSH

Here we go round the mul-berry bush, the mul-berry bush, the

mul-berry bush, Here we go round the mul-berry bush All

Here we go round the mulberry bush,
   the mulberry bush, the mulberry bush,
Here we go round the mulberry bush
   All on a frosty morning.

1 This is the way we clap our hands,
    this is the way we clap our hands,
This is the way we clap our hands
   All on a frosty morning.
Here we go round the mulberry bush, &c.

2 This is the way we stamp our feet,

3 This is the way we wash our face,

4 This is the way we brush our hair,

5 This is the way we go to bed,

6 This is the way we get up again,

7 This is the way we dance about,

SEE-SAW,
MARGERY DAW

See - saw, Mar - ge - ry Daw,

Sold her bed to lie up-on straw; Was - n't she a

dir - ty slut To sell her bed and lie up-on dirt?

See-saw, Margery Daw,
Sold her bed to lie upon straw;
Wasn't she a dirty slut
To sell her bed and lie upon dirt?

RIDE A COCK-HORSE

Ride a cock-horse to Ban-bu-ry Cross, To

see a fine la-dy up-on a white horse;

Rings on her fin-gers and bells on her toes, And

she shall have mu - sic where - e - ver she goes.

Ride a cock-horse to Banbury Cross,
To see a fine lady upon a white horse;
Rings on her fingers and bells on her toes,
And she shall have music wherever she goes.

THE FROG AND THE CROW

1 A jol - ly fat frog lived in the ri - ver swim, O! A come - ly black crow lived on the ri - ver brim, O! Come on shore, come on shore, Said the crow to the frog, and then, O! No, you'll bite me, no, you'll

bite me, Said the frog to the crow a - gain, O!

1   A jolly fat frog lived in the river swim, O!
A comely black crow lived on the river brim, O!
   Come on shore, come on shore,
Said the crow to the frog, and then, O!
   No, you'll bite me, no, you'll bite me,
Said the frog to the crow again, O!

2   O there is sweet music on yonder green hill, O!
And you shall be a dancer, a dancer in yellow,
   All in yellow, all in yellow,
Said the crow to the frog, and then, O!
   All in yellow, all in yellow,
Said the frog to the crow again, O!

3   Farewell, ye little fishes that in the river swim, O!
I'm going to be a dancer, a dancer in yellow.
   O beware! O beware!
Said the fish to the frog, and then, O!
   I'll take care, I'll take care,
Said the frog to the fish again, O!

4   The frog began a-swimming, a-swimming to land, O!
And the crow began jumping to give him his hand, O!
   Sir, you're welcome, Sir, you're welcome,
Said the crow to the frog, and then, O!
   Sir, I thank you, Sir, I thank you,
Said the frog to the crow again, O!

5   But where is the sweet music on yonder green hill, O!
And where are all the dancers, the dancers in yellow?
   All in yellow, all in yellow?
Said the frog to the crow, and then, O!
   Sir, they're here, Sir, they're here,
Said the crow to the frog—*

*Here the crow swallows the frog

POLLY PUT THE KETTLE ON

1 Pol - ly put the ket - tle on, Pol - ly put the ket - tle on,

Pol - ly put the ket - tle on, We'll all have tea.

2 Su - key take it off a - gain, Su - key take it off a - gain,

Su - key take it off a - gain, They've all gone a - way.

1 Polly put the kettle on,
Polly put the kettle on,
Polly put the kettle on,
   We'll all have tea.

2 Sukey take it off again,
Sukey take it off again,
Sukey take it off again,
   They've all gone away.

SUR
LE PONT
D'AVIGNON

ON THE BRIDGE OF AVIGNON

Sur le pont d'A - vi - gnon, L'on y dan - se, l'on y
On the bridge, on the bridge, See them dan - cing, see them

dan - se, Sur le pont d'A - vi - gnon, L'on y dan - se tout en rond. 1 Les
dan - cing, On the bridge, on the bridge, On the bridge at A - vi - gnon. 1 The

beaux mes - sieurs font comm' ci, Et puis en - core comm'
gen - tle - men bow this way, Then a - gain bow that

ça. Sur le pont d'A - vi - gnon, L'on y dan - se, l'on y
way. On the bridge, on the bridge, See them dan - cing, see them

dan - se, Sur le pont d'A - vi - gnon, L'on y dan - se tout en rond.
dan - cing, On the bridge, on the bridge, On the bridge at A - vi - gnon.

Sur le pont d'Avignon,	On the bridge, on the bridge,
L'on y danse, l'on y danse,	See them dancing, see them dancing,
Sur le pont d'Avignon,	On the bridge, on the bridge,
L'on y danse tout en rond.	On the bridge at Avignon.

1 Les beaux messieurs font comm' ci,
Et puis encore comm' ça.
Sur le pont, &c.

1 The gentlemen bow this way,
Then again bow that way.
On the bridge, &c.

2 Les belles dames font comm' ci,
Et puis encore comm' ça.
Sur le pont, &c.

2 The ladies curtsey this way,
Then they curtsey that way.
On the bridge, &c.

3 Les soldats font comm' ci,
Et puis encore comm' ça.
Sur le pont, &c.

3 The soldiers salute this way,
Then they salute that way.
On the bridge, &c.

4 Les capucines font comm' ci,
Et puis encore comm' ça.
Sur le pont, &c.

4 The monks and nuns pray this way,
Then again pray that way.
On the bridge, &c.

5 Les gamins font comm' ci,
Et puis encore comm' ça.
Sur le pont, &c.

5 The children all play this way,
And again play that way.
On the bridge, &c.

ORANGES AND LEMONS

1 Oran-ges and le-mons, Say the bells of St Cle-ment's. 2 You owe me five far-things, Say the bells of St Mar-tin's. 3 When will you pay me? Say the bells of Old Bai-ley. 4 When I grow rich, Say the bells of Shore-ditch. 5 When will that be? Say the bells of Step-

ney. 6 I do not know, Says the great bell of Bow.

Here comes a can-dle to__ light you to bed, And

here comes a chop-per to__ chop off your head.

1 Oranges and lemons,
   Say the bells of St Clement's.

2 You owe me five farthings,
   Say the bells of St Martin's.

3 When will you pay me?
   Say the bells of Old Bailey.

4 When I grow rich,
   Say the bells of Shoreditch.

5 When will that be?
   Say the bells of Stepney.

6 I do not know,
   Says the great bell of Bow.

Here comes a candle to light you to bed,
And here comes a chopper to chop off your head.

OH DEAR, WHAT
CAN THE MATTER BE?

Oh dear, what can the mat-ter be? Oh dear,

what can the mat-ter be? Oh dear, what can the mat-ter be?

Fine

John-ny's so long at the fair. 1 He pro-mised to buy me a

bunch of blue rib-bons, He pro-mised to buy me a

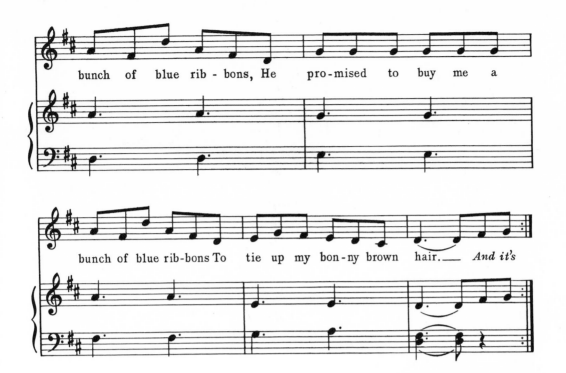

bunch of blue rib - bons, He pro-mised to buy me a

bunch of blue rib-bons To tie up my bon-ny brown hair.___ *And it's*

Oh dear, what can the matter be?
Oh dear, what can the matter be?
Oh dear, what can the matter be?
Johnny's so long at the fair.

1 He promised to buy me a bunch of blue ribbons,
He promised to buy me a bunch of blue ribbons,
He promised to buy me a bunch of blue ribbons
To tie up my bonny brown hair.

And it's oh dear, what can the matter be?
Oh dear, what can the matter be?
Oh dear, what can the matter be?
Johnny's so long at the fair.

2 He promised he'd bring me a basket of posies,
A garland of lilies, a garland of roses,
A little straw hat, to set off the blue ribbons
That tie up my bonny brown hair.

And it's oh dear, what can the matter be?
Oh dear, what can the matter be?
Oh dear, what can the matter be?
Johnny's so long at the fair.

THREE BLIND MICE

Three blind mice, three blind mice,

See how_ they run! see how_ they run! They

all ran af-ter the farm-er's wife, Who cut off their tails with a

car - ving knife; Did e - ver you see such a

thing in your life, As three blind mice?

Three blind mice, three blind mice,
See how they run! see how they run!
They all ran after the farmer's wife,
Who cut off their tails with a carving knife;
Did ever you see such a thing in your life,
     As three blind mice?

LUCY LOCKET

Lu — cy Lock — et lost her pock — et,

Kit — ty Fish — er found it; But not a pen — ny

was there in it, But the bind — ing round it.

Lucy Locket lost her pocket,
Kitty Fisher found it;
But not a penny was there in it,
But the binding round it.

MADAMA DORÉ

© Elizabeth Poston 1971
Words and tune coll. E.P.

1 O quan-te bel - le fi-glie, Ma-da-ma Do -
1 How ma - ny love - ly daugh-ters, Ma-da-ma Do -

ré, O quan-te bel - le fi - glie!_____
ré, How ma - ny love - ly daugh - ters!_____

1   O quante belle figlie,
          Madama Doré,
  O quante belle figlie!

2   Che cosa ne vuoi fare?
          Madama Doré,
  Che cosa ne vuoi fare?

3   Le voglio maritare,
          Madama Doré,
  Le voglio maritare.

4   Scegliete chi vi pare,
          Madama Doré,
  Scegliete chi vi pare.

5   La più bella che sia,
          Madama Doré,
  La più bella che sia.

6   Me la voglio portar' via,
          Madama Doré,
  Me la voglio portar' via.

1   How many lovely daughters,
          Madama Doré,
  How many lovely daughters!

2   O what will you do with them?
          Madama Doré,
  O what will you do with them?

3   I want them all to marry,
          Madama Doré,
  I want them all to marry.

4   Then choose the one you fancy,
          Madama Doré,
  Then choose the one you fancy.

5   The prettiest one I fancy,
          Madama Doré,
  The prettiest one I fancy.

6   I'm going to take her with me,
          Madama Doré,
  I'm going to take her with me.

HUSH-A-BYE BABY

Hush - a - bye ba - by, on the tree top,

When the wind blows, the cra - dle will rock;

When the bough breaks, the cra - dle will fall —

Down comes ba - by, cra - dle and all.

Hush-a-bye baby, on the tree top,
When the wind blows, the cradle will rock;
When the bough breaks, the cradle will fall—
Down comes baby, cradle and all.

THREE LITTLE KITTENS

1 There were three lit - tle kit - tens Put on their mit - tens, To eat some Christ - mas pie.

1-4 *Mew, mew, Mew, mew, Mew, mew, mew._____*
5 *Purr - rr, purr - rr, Purr - rr - rr._____*

1   There were three little kittens
Put on their mittens,
To eat some Christmas pie.
Mew, mew, Mew, mew,
Mew, mew, mew.

2   These three little kittens
They lost their mittens,
And all began to cry.
Mew, mew, Mew, mew,
Mew, mew, mew.

3   Go, go, naughty kittens,
And find your mittens,
Or you shan't have any pie.
Mew, mew, Mew, mew,
Mew, mew, mew.

4   These three little kittens
They found their mittens,
And joyfully they did cry:
Mew, mew, Mew, mew,
Mew, mew, mew.

5   O Granny, dear!
Our mittens are here,
Make haste and cut up the pie!
Purr-rr, purr-rr,
Purr-rr-rr.

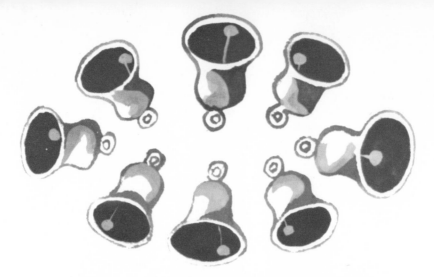

MY LADY'S GARDEN

How does my la - dy's gar - den grow?

How does my la - dy's gar - den grow? With

sil - ver bells and coc - kle shells, And

pret - ty maids all in a row. ———

How does my lady's garden grow?
How does my lady's garden grow?
With silver bells and cockle shells,
And pretty maids all in a row.

SKIP TO MY LOU

1 Skip, skip, skip to my Lou, Skip, skip, skip to my Lou, Skip, skip, skip to my Lou, Skip to my Lou, my dar - ling.

1   Skip, skip, skip to my Lou,
     Skip, skip, skip to my Lou,
     Skip, skip, skip to my Lou,
       Skip to my Lou, my darling.

2   Partner's gone, what will I do?
     Partner's gone, what will I do?
     Partner's gone, what will I do?
       Skip to my Lou, my darling.
       Skip, skip, &c.

SCHLAF, KINDLEIN, SCHLAF

SLEEP, BABY, SLEEP

1 Schlaf, Kind-lein, schlaf! Der Va - ter hütt't die
1 Sleep, ba - by, sleep! Your fa - ther keeps the

Schaf, Die Mut - ter schüt - telt's Bäu - me - lein, da
sheep, Your mo - ther shakes the lit - tle bough, a

fällt her - ab ein Träu-me-lein. Schlaf, Kind-lein, schlaf!
dream falls gent - ly on you now. Sleep, ba - by, sleep!

1   Schlaf, Kindlein, schlaf!
    Der Vater hütt't die Schaf,
    Die Mutter schüttelt's Bäumelein,
    da fällt herab ein Träumelein.
    Schlaf, Kindlein, schlaf!

2   Schlaf, Kindlein, schlaf!
    Dein Papa hüt' die Schaf;
    Deine Mutter hüt' die Lämmerchen,
    bei den lieben Engelchen.
    Schlaf, Kindlein, schlaf!

3   Schlaf, Kindlein, schlaf!
    Am Himmel wandern d'Schaf,
    Die Stern die sind die Lämmerle,
    Der Mond der ist das Schäferle.
    Schlaf, Kindlein, schlaf!

1   Sleep, baby, sleep!
    Your father keeps the sheep,
    Your mother shakes the little bough,
    a dream falls gently on you now.
    Sleep, baby, sleep!

2   Sleep, baby, sleep!
    Your daddy keeps the sheep,
    Your mother keeps the little lambs
    beside her little angel lamb.
    Sleep, baby, sleep!

3   Sleep, baby, sleep!
    In heaven browse the sheep,
    The little lambs are stars of gold,
    The moon's the shepherd of the fold.
    Sleep, baby, sleep!

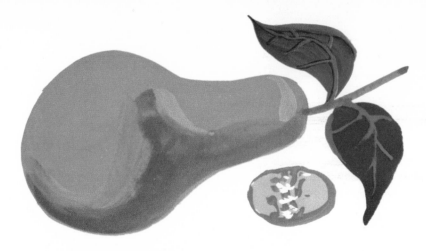

I HAD A LITTLE NUT TREE

© Elizabeth Poston 1971

I had a lit-tle nut tree, No-thing would it bear

But a sil-ver nut-meg And a gold-en pear; The

King of Spain's daugh-ter Came to vi-sit me, And

all— for the sake Of my lit-tle nut tree.

I had a little nut tree,
  Nothing would it bear
But a silver nutmeg
  And a golden pear;
The King of Spain's daughter
  Came to visit me,
And all for the sake
  Of my little nut tree.

HOT-CROSS BUNS!

Hot - cross Buns!   Hot - cross Buns!   One a pen - ny, two a pen - ny,

Hot - cross Buns!   Hot - cross Buns!   Hot - cross Buns!

If your daugh-ters do not like them, Give them to your sons.

If you have no daugh - ters,   If you have no daugh - ters,

If you have no daugh - ters,— Give them to your sons; But if you have - n't a - ny of these pret - ty lit - tle elves, Then— you must eat— them— all your - selves.

Hot-cross Buns!
Hot-cross Buns!
One a penny, two a penny,
    Hot-cross Buns!

Hot-cross Buns!
Hot-cross Buns!
If your daughters do not like them,
    Give them to your sons.

If you have no daughters,   (*three times*)
    Give them to your sons;
But if you haven't any of these pretty little elves,
    Then you must eat them all yourselves.

BAA, BAA, BLACK SHEEP

Baa, baa, black sheep, Have you a - ny wool? Yes, sir,

yes, sir, Three bags full; One for the mas - ter, And

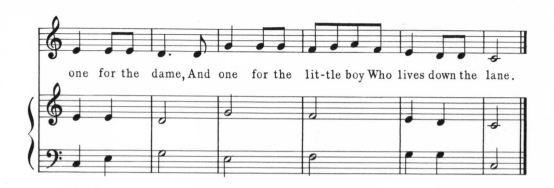

one for the dame, And one for the lit-tle boy Who lives down the lane.

Baa, baa, black sheep,
    Have you any wool?
Yes, sir, yes, sir,
    Three bags full;
One for the master,
    And one for the dame,
And one for the little boy
    Who lives down the lane.

AIKEN DRUM

1 There_ was a man lived in the moon, lived

in the moon, lived in the moon, There_ was a man lived

in the moon, And his name was Ai - ken Drum; And he

played up - on a la - dle, a la - dle, a la - dle, And he

played up - on a la - dle, And his name was Ai - ken Drum.

1 There was a man lived in the moon,
  lived in the moon, lived in the moon,
  There was a man lived in the moon,
  And his name was Aiken Drum;
  And he played upon a ladle,
  a ladle, a ladle,
  And he played upon a ladle,
  And his name was Aiken Drum.

2 And his hat was made of good cream cheese,
  And his name, &c.

3 And his coat was made of good roast beef,
  And his name, &c.

4 And his buttons were made of penny loaves,
  And his name, &c.

5 His waistcoat was made of crust of pies,
  And his name, &c.

6 His breeches were made of haggis bags,
  And his name, &c.

7 There was a man in another town,
  And his name was Willy Wood;
  And he played upon a razor,
  And his name was Willy Wood.

8 And he ate up all the good cream cheese,
  And his name, &c.

9 And he ate up all the good roast beef,
  And his name, &c.

10 And he ate up all the penny loaves,
  And his name, &c.

11 And he ate up all the good pie crust,
  And his name, &c.

12 But he choked upon the haggis bags,
  And that ended Willy Wood.

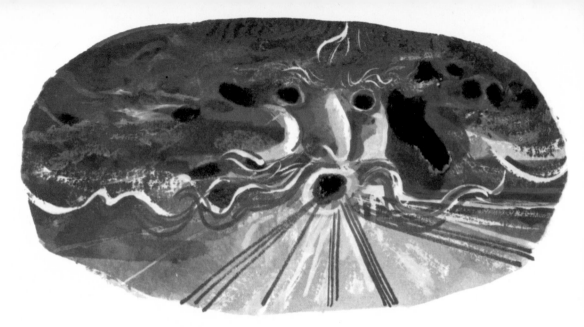

THE NORTH WIND

The north wind doth blow,— And we shall have snow, And what will poor Ro-bin do then, poor thing? He'll sit in a barn— And keep him-self warm, And

hide his head un - der his wing, poor thing.

The north wind doth blow,
And we shall have snow,
And what will poor Robin do then, poor thing?
He'll sit in a barn
And keep himself warm,
And hide his head under his wing, poor thing.

RING-A-RING O' ROSES

Ring - a - ring o' ro - ses, A po - cket full of po - sies, A - tish - oo! A - tish - oo! We all fall down.

Ring-a-ring o' roses,
A pocket full of posies,
A-tishoo! A-tishoo!
We all fall down.

DERRIERE DE CHEZ MON PERE

MY FATHER'S APPLE TREE

Acc. © Elizabeth Poston 1971

1 Der - rièr' de chez mon pè - re, Lan la, lan - di - gue da,
1 Back there, be-hind my fa-ther's, Lon la, lon - dig - ga da,

Der - rièr' de chez mon pè - re, Lan la, lan - di - gue da,
Back there, be-hind my fa-ther's, Lon la, lon - dig - ga da,

Un pom-mier il y a, *Lan - di - gue - di - gue lan lir',*
There is an ap-ple tree, Lon - dig - ga - dig - ga lon lir,

Un pom-mier il y a, Lan-di-gue-di-gue lan lir'.
There is an ap-ple tree, Lon-dig-ga-dig-ga lon lir.

1 Derrière de chez mon père, *Lan la, landigue da,* Derrière de chez mon père, *Lan la, landigue da,* Un pommier il y a, *Landiguedigue lan lire,* Un pommier il y a, *Landiguedigue lan lire.*	1 Back there, behind my father's, *Lon la, londigga da,* Back there, behind my father's, *Lon la, londigga da,* There is an apple tree, *Londiggadigga lon lir,* There is an apple tree, *Londiggadigga lon lir.*
2 Il y a autant de pommes, *Lan la, landigue da,* Il y a autant de pommes, *Lan la, landigue da,* Que de feuilles il y a, *Landiguedigue lan lire,* Que de feuilles il y a, *Landiguedigue lan lire.*	2 It is as full of apples, *Lon la, londigga da,* It is as full of apples, *Lon la, londigga da,* As it is full of leaves, *Londiggadigga lon lir,* As it is full of leaves, *Londiggadigga lon lir.*
3 Mad'leine d'mande à son père, *Lan la, landigue da,* Mad'leine d'mande à son père, *Lan la, landigue da,* Quand on les cueillera, *Landiguedigue lan lire,* Quand on les cueillera, *Landiguedigue lan lire.*	3 Mad'leine she asks her father, *Lon la, londigga da,* Mad'leine she asks her father, *Lon la, londigga da,* When picking time will be, *Londiggadigga lon lir,* When picking time will be, *Londiggadigga lon lir.*
4 A la Saint-Jean, ma fille, *Lan la, landigue da,* A la Saint-Jean, ma fille, *Lan la, landigue da,* Quand la saison sera, *Landiguedigue lan lire,* Quand la saison sera, *Landiguedigue lan lire.*	4 Saint-John, midsummer, daughter, *Lon la, londigga da,* Saint-John, midsummer, daughter, *Lon la, londigga da,* That's when they picked will be, *Londiggadigga lon lir,* That's when they picked will be, *Londiggadigga lon lir.*

from Edmée Arma: *Entrez dans la Danse*.
Henry Lemoine et Cie, Paris. By permission.

PUSSY CAT, PUSSY CAT, WHERE HAVE YOU BEEN?

Pus - sy cat, pus - sy cat, where have you been?

I've been to Lon - don to look at the queen

Pus - sy cat, pus - sy cat, what did you there?

I caught a lit - tle mouse un - der her chair.

Pussy cat, pussy cat, where have you been?
I've been to London to look at the queen.
Pussy cat, pussy cat, what did you there?
I caught a little mouse under her chair.

OLD KING COLE

1 Old King Cole was a mer-ry old__ soul, And a mer-ry old soul was he; He__ called for his pipe, And he called for his bowl, And he called for his fid - dlers__ three.

2 Old King Cole
   Was a merry old soul,
   And a merry old soul was he;
   He called for his pipe,
   And he called for his bowl,
   And he called for his harpers three.
   Ev'ry harper he had a fine harp,
   And a very fine harp had he:
   Twang-a-twang, twang-a-twang,
     twang-a-twang, twang-a-twang,
   Tweedle dee, tweedle dee,
     tweedle dee, tweedle dee,
   O there's none so rare
   As can compare
   With King Cole and his fiddlers three.

3 Old King Cole
   Was a merry old soul,
   And a merry old soul was he;
   He called for his pipe,
   And he called for his bowl,
   And he called for his pipers three.
   Ev'ry piper he had a fine pipe,
   And a very fine pipe had he:
   Tootle too, tootle too, tootle too, tootle too,
   Twang-a-twang, twang-a-twang,
     twang-a-twang, twang-a-twang,
   Tweedle dee, tweedle dee,
     tweedle dee, tweedle dee,
   O there's none so rare
   As can compare
   With King Cole and his fiddlers three.

OH, WHAT HAVE YOU GOT
FOR DINNER, MRS BOND?

© Elizabeth Poston 1971

1 Oh,—— what have you got for dinner, Mis-sis Bond? There's beef— in the lar - der, and ducks— in the pond; Dil - ly, dil - ly,

dil - ly, dil - ly, come— to be killed, For you— must be stuffed and my cus - to - mers filled.

1 Oh, what have you got for dinner, Mrs Bond?
   There's beef in the larder, and ducks in the pond;
   Dilly, dilly, dilly, dilly, come to be killed,
   For you must be stuffed and my customers filled.

2 John Ostler, go fetch me a duckling or two,
   Ma'am, says John Ostler, I'll try what I can do;
   Cry, Dilly, dilly, dilly, dilly, come to be killed,
   For you must be stuffed and my customers filled.

3 I have been to the ducks that swim in the pond,
   But I found they won't come to be killed, Mrs Bond;
   I cried, Dilly, dilly, dilly, dilly, come to be killed,
   For you must be stuffed and my customers filled.

4 Mrs Bond she went down to the pond in a rage,
   With plenty of onions and plenty of sage;
   She cried, Come, little wag-tails, come to be killed,
   For you must be stuffed and my customers filled.

E ARRIVATO L'AMBASCIATORE
HERE'S THE AMBASSADOR, HE'S ARRIVING

© Elizabeth Poston 1971
Words and tune coll. E.P.

1 E ar - ri - va - to l'am - ba - scia - to - re di suoi
1 Here's the am - bas - sa - dor, he's ar - riv - ing from his

mon - ti e dal - le val - li; E ar - ri - va - to l'am - ba - scia -
moun-tains and by the val - leys; O the am - bas - sa - dor he's ar -

1 E arrivato l'ambasciatore
    di suoi monti e dalle valli;
    E arrivato l'ambasciatore.
    A-io-là, io-là, io-là.
	1 Here's the ambassador, he's arriving
	    from his mountains and by the valleys;
	    O the ambassador he's arriving.
	    A-io-là, io-là, io-là.

2 Che cosa vuole, l'ambasciatore?
    di suoi monti e dalle valli;
    Che cosa vuole, l'ambasciatore?
    A-io-là, io-là, io-là.
	2 What are Excellency's wishes?
	    from his mountains and by the valleys;
	    What are his Excellency's wishes?
	    A-io-là, io-là, io-là.

3 Noi vogliamo una bimba bella
    di suoi monti e dalle valli;
    Noi vogliamo una bimba bella.
    A-io-là, io-là, io-là.
	3 A fair girl is what we're asking
	    from his mountains and by the valleys;
	    A fair girl is what we're asking.
	    A-io-là, io-là, io-là.

4 E come la vestirete?	4 Now we've brought her, how shall we dress her?
5 La vestiremo di pelle d'oca.	5 We will dress her all in a goose skin.
6 Ora no, non siam' contenti.	6 That won't do; we won't accept it.
7 La vestiremo con un vestito di brillianti.	7 Then, we'll give her a dress of diamonds.
8 Ora si, che siam' contenti.	8 That is fitting; we're quite content now.

9 Ecco gli sposi che vanno
    a marito,
    Con due gento anelli in dito;
    Cento di qua, cento di là,
    Ecco gli sposi che sene van'.
	9 Here are the bridegrooms, who come
	    a-singing,
	    Two attendants the gold rings bringing;
	    A hundred here, and a hundred there,
	    Then to church they're off, they'll soon
	    be there.

10 Se ne vanno a Santa Croce,
    Ecco gli sposi che schiaccian'
    le noce;
    E ne schiaccian' due a tre,
    Ecco gli sposi che vanno
    a seder'.
	10 It's to Holy Cross they're going,
	    Cracking nuts, that's what they're doing;
	    They'll be cracking them round the town,
	    And now the bridegrooms all sit down.

MERRILY DANCE
THE QUAKER'S WIFE

© Elizabeth Poston 1971

Mer-ri-ly dance the Quaker's wife,

Mer-ri-ly dance the Quaker; Mer-ri-ly dance the

Qua-ker's wife, Mer-ri-ly dance the Qua-ker.

She was a semp-stress all her life,

He was an un - der - tak - er; Mer - ri - ly dance— the

Qua - ker's wife, Mer - ri - ly dance the Qua - ker.

Merrily dance the Quaker's wife,
   Merrily dance the Quaker;
Merrily dance the Quaker's wife,
   Merrily dance the Quaker.
She was a sempstress all her life,
   He was an undertaker;
Merrily dance the Quaker's wife,
   Merrily dance the Quaker.

LAVENDER'S BLUE

1 La - ven - der's blue, did - dle did - dle,
La - ven - der's green; When I am
king, did - dle did - dle, You shall be queen.

1 Lavender's blue, diddle diddle, 2 Call up your men, diddle diddle,
  Lavender's green;   Set them to work;
When I am king, diddle diddle,   Some to the plough, diddle diddle,
  You shall be queen.   Some to the cart.

    3 Some to make hay, diddle diddle,
      Some to cut corn;
   While you and I, diddle diddle,
     Keep ourselves warm.

JACK AND JILL

Jack and Jill went up the hill To fetch a pail of wa - ter; Jack fell down and broke his crown, And

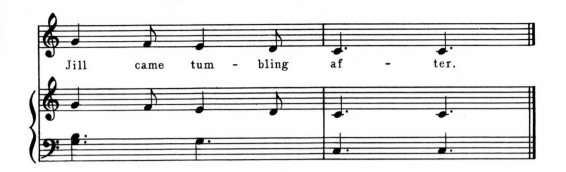

Jill came tum - bling af - ter.

Jack and Jill went up the hill
  To fetch a pail of water;
Jack fell down and broke his crown,
  And Jill came tumbling after.

WIDEWIDEWENNE
BIDDY BIDDY BURKEY

1 Wi - de - wi - de - wen - ne heisst mei - ne Trut -
1 Bid - dy Bid - dy Bur - key's the name of my

hen - ne, Kann - nicht - ruhn heisst mein Huhn,
tur - key, Dash - ing Dick he's my chick,

We - del-schwanz heisst mei - ne Gans; Wi - de - wi - de -
Lop - tail - loose, there goes my goose; Bid - dy Bid - dy

wen - ne heisst mei - ne Trut - hen - ne.
Bur - key's the name of my tur - key.

Widewidewenne heisst meine Trut-henne,
Kann-nicht-ruhn heisst mein Huhn,
Wedelschwanz heisst meine Gans;
Widewidewenne heisst meine Trut-henne.

Widewidewenne heisst meine Trut-henne,
Entequent heisst meine Ent',
Sammetmatz heisst meine Katz;
Widewidewenne heisst meine Trut-henne.

Widewidewenne heisst meine Trut-henne,
Schwarz und weiss heisst meine Geiss,
Schmortöpflein heisst mein Schwein;
Widewidewenne heisst meine Trut-henne.

1 Biddy Biddy Burkey's the name of my turkey,
Dashing Dick he's my chick,
Loptail-loose, there goes my goose;
Biddy Biddy Burkey's the name of my turkey.

2 Biddy Biddy Burkey's the name of my turkey,
Quickquackquuck she's my duck,
Pusspitpat, there goes my cat;
Biddy Biddy Burkey's the name of my turkey.

3 Biddy Biddy Burkey's the name of my turkey,
White-'n'-black-coat he's my goat,
Tuck-pot-tig, there goes my pig;
Biddy Biddy Burkey's the name of my turkey.

THE LITTLE COCK SPARROW

1 A little cock spar-row sat on a green tree, And he chir-rupped, he chir-rupped, so mer-ry was he; A little cock spar-row sat on a green tree, And he chir-rupped, he chir-rupped, so mer-ry was he; He chir-rupped, he chir-rupped, he chir-rupped, he chir-rupped, He

chir-rupped, he chir-rupped, he chir-rupped, he chir-rupped, A lit-tle cock spar-row sat

on a green tree, And he chir-rupped, he chir-rupped, so mer-ry was he.

1   A little cock sparrow sat on a green tree,
    And he chirrupped, he chirrupped, so merry was he; *(twice)*
    He chirrupped, he chirrupped, he chirrupped, he chirrupped,
    He chirrupped, he chirrupped, he chirrupped, he chirrupped,
    A little cock sparrow sat on a green tree,
    And he chirrupped, he chirrupped, so merry was he.

2   A naughty boy came with his wee bow and arrow,
    Says he, I will shoot this little cock sparrow; *(twice)*
    I will shoot, I will shoot, I will shoot, I will shoot,
    I will shoot, I will shoot, I will shoot, I will shoot,
    A naughty boy came with his wee bow and arrow,
    Says he, I will shoot this little cock sparrow.

3   His body will make me a nice little stew,
    And his giblets will make me a little pie too; *(twice)*
    His giblets, his giblets, his giblets, his giblets,
    His giblets, his giblets, his giblets, his giblets,
    His body will make me a nice little stew,
    And his giblets will make me a little pie too.

4   Oh, no, said the sparrow, I won't make a stew,
    So he fluttered his wings and away he flew; *(twice)*
    He fluttered, he fluttered, he fluttered, he fluttered,
    He fluttered, he fluttered, he fluttered, he fluttered,
    Oh, no, said the sparrow, I won't make a stew,
    So he fluttered his wings and away he flew.

TOM, THE PIPER'S SON

Tom, Tom, the pi-per's son Stole a___ pig and a-
way he run; The pig was eat And Tom was beat, And
Tom went___ roar-ing down the street.

Tom, Tom, the piper's son
Stole a pig and away he run;
   The pig was eat
    And Tom was beat,
And Tom went roaring down the street.

THE OLD WOMAN
AND THE PEDLAR

1 There was a lit-tle wo-man, As I've heard tell, She went to mar-ket, Her eggs for to sell; *Fol, lol, did-dle did-dle dol;* She went to mar-ket All on a mar-ket day, And she fell a-sleep Up-on the king's high-way. *Fol de rol de lol lol lol lol lol, Fol, lol, did-dle did-dle dol.*

1 There was a little woman,
   As I've heard tell,
       Fol, lol, diddle diddle dol;
   She went to market,
   Her eggs for to sell;
       Fol, lol, diddle diddle dol;
   She went to market
   All on a market day,
   And she fell asleep
   Upon the king's highway.
       Fol de rol de lol lol lol lol lol,
       Fol, lol, diddle diddle dol.

2 There came by a pedlar,
   His name was Stout,
       Fol, lol, diddle diddle dol;
   He cut her petticoats
   All round about;
       Fol, lol, diddle diddle dol;
   He cut her petticoats
   Up to the knees,
   Which made the little woman
   To shiver and sneeze.
       Fol de rol de lol lol lol lol lol,
       Fol, lol, diddle diddle dol.

3 When the little woman
   Began to awake,
       Fol, lol, diddle diddle dol;
   She began to shiver,
   And she began to shake;
       Fol, lol, diddle diddle dol;
   She began to shake,
   And she began to cry,
   Lawk-a-mercy on me!
   This is none of I.
       Fol de rol de lol lol lol lol lol,
       Fol, lol, diddle diddle dol.

4 If this be I,
   As I hope it be,
       Fol, lol, diddle diddle dol;
   I've a little dog at home
   And he knows me;
       Fol, lol, diddle diddle dol;
   If it be I,
   He will wag his little tail,
   If it be not I,
   He will bark and rail.
       Fol de rol de lol lol lol lol lol,
       Fol, lol, diddle diddle dol.

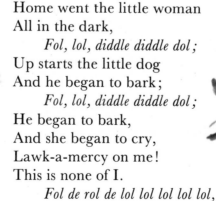

5 Home went the little woman
   All in the dark,
       Fol, lol, diddle diddle dol;
   Up starts the little dog
   And he began to bark;
       Fol, lol, diddle diddle dol;
   He began to bark,
   And she began to cry,
   Lawk-a-mercy on me!
   This is none of I.
       Fol de rol de lol lol lol lol lol,
       Fol, lol, diddle diddle dol.

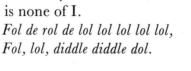

LITTLE MISS MUFFET

Lit - tle Miss Muf - fet Sat on a tuf - fet,

Eat - ing her curds and whey; _____ There

came a big spi - der Who sat down be - side her, And

fright-ened Miss Muf-fet a - way.

Little Miss Muffet
Sat on a tuffet,
Eating her curds and whey;
There came a big spider
Who sat down beside her,
And frightened Miss Muffet away.

PRETTY LITTLE HORSES

1 Hush you bye, Don't you cry, Go to sleep-y, lit-tle ba — by; When you wake, You shall have cake, And drive those pret-ty lit-tle hor — ses.

1   Hush you bye,
     Don't you cry,
     Go to sleepy, little baby;
     When you wake,
     You shall have cake,
     And drive those pretty little horses.

2   Hush you bye,
     Don't you cry,
     Go to sleepy, little baby;
     Blacks and bays,
     Dapples and grays,
     And coach and six-a little horses.

SAN SERENI DEL MONTE
SAINT SERENI OF THE MOUNTAIN

1 San Se - re - ní del mon - te, San Se - re -

1 Saint Se - re - ní of the moun - tain, court - eous and

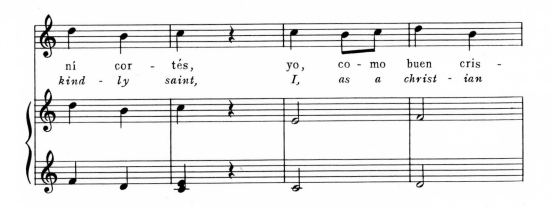

ní cor - tés, yo, co - mo buen cris -
kind - ly saint, *I,* *as a christ - ian*

tia - no, yo me a - rro - di - lla - ré.
child, *I'll kneel me____ down to pray.*

1 San Sereni del monte,
San Sereni cortés,
yo, como buen cristiano,
yo me arrodillaré.

1 Saint Sereni of the mountain,
courteous and kindly saint,
I, as a christian child,
I'll kneel me down to pray.

2 San Sereni del monte,
San Sereni cortés,
yo, como buen cristiano,
yo me sentaré.

2 Saint Sereni of the mountain,
courteous and kindly saint,
I, as a christian child,
I'll sit me down from play.

3 San Sereni del monte,
San Sereni cortés,
yo, como buen cristiano,
yo me echaré.

3 Saint Sereni of the mountain,
courteous and kindly saint,
I, as a christian child,
I'll stretch me down to lay.

4 San Sereni del monte,
San Sereni cortés,
yo, como buen cristiano,
yo me levantaré.

4 Saint Sereni of the mountain,
courteous and kindly saint,
I, as a christian child,
I'll get me up at day.

WHERE ARE YOU GOING TO,
MY PRETTY MAID?

1 Where are you going to, my pret-ty maid?
Where are you going to, my pret-ty maid? I'm

go - ing a - milk - ing, sir, she said, Sir, she said,

sir, she said, I'm go - ing a - milk - ing, sir, she said.

1 Where are you going to, my pretty maid?
   Where are you going to, my pretty maid?
   I'm going a-milking, sir, she said,
   Sir, she said, sir, she said,
   I'm going a-milking, sir, she said.

3 Say, will you marry me, my pretty maid?
   Say, will you marry me, my pretty maid?
   Yes, if you please, kind sir, she said,
   Sir, she said, sir, she said,
   Yes, if you please, kind sir, she said.

2 May I go with you, my pretty maid?
   May I go with you, my pretty maid?
   Yes, if you please, kind sir, she said,
   Sir, she said, sir, she said,
   Yes, if you please, kind sir, she said.

4 What is your fortune, my pretty maid?
   What is your fortune, my pretty maid?
   My face is my fortune, sir, she said,
   Sir, she said, sir, she said,
   My face is my fortune, sir, she said.

5 Then I can't marry you, my pretty maid,
   Then I can't marry you, my pretty maid.
   Nobody asked you, sir, she said,
   Sir, she said, sir, she said,
   Nobody asked you, sir, she said.

GOOD KING ARTHUR

1 When good King Ar - thur ruled this land, He

was a good - ly king; He stole three pecks of

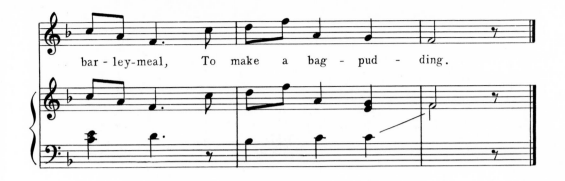

bar - ley-meal, To make a bag - pud - ding.

1 When good King Arthur ruled this land,
   He was a goodly king;
   He stole three pecks of barley-meal,
   To make a bag-pudding.

2 A bag-pudding the king did make,
   And stuffed it well with plums;
   And in it put great lumps of fat,
   As big as my two thumbs.

3 The king and queen did eat thereof,
   The noblemen beside;
   And what they could not eat that night,
   The queen next morning fried.

RINGELTANZ
ROUND DANCE

© Elizabeth Poston 1971

Es reg-net auf der Brü - cke, und es werd nass. Ich
Up - on the bridge it's rain - ing, and we'll get wet. There's

hab' et - was ver - ges - sen, und weiss nicht was. Ach,
some-thing I've for - got - ten, what is it yet? O

schön-ster Schatz, komm' 'rein zu mir, es sind kein schön - 're
pret - ty one, come in with me, there's none so sweet as

Es regnet auf der Brücke, und es werd nass.
Ich hab' etwas vergessen, und weiss nicht was.
    Ach, schönster Schatz, komm' 'rein zu mir,
    es sind kein schön're Leut' als wir.
Ei, ja, freilich!
Wer ich bin, der bleib ich,
bleib' ich wer ich bin:
Adje, adje! mein Kind!

Upon the bridge it's raining, and we'll get wet.
There's something I've forgotten, what is it yet?
    O pretty one, come in with me,
    there's none so sweet as mermaids free.
Say O, say O,
Who I am, I stay O,
who I am, I stay:
And so to you, good day!

GEORGIE PORGIE

Geor - gie Por - gie pud-ding and pie, Kissed the girls_ and

made them cry; When the boys_ came out to play, _

Georgie Porgie pudding and pie,
Kissed the girls and made them cry;
When the boys came out to play,
Georgie Porgie ran away.

COCK ROBIN AND JENNY WREN

1 'Twas on a mer-ry time, When Jen-ny Wren was young, So neat-ly as she danced, And so sweet-ly as she sung; Ro-bin Red-breast lost his heart, He

was a gal - lant bird, He doffed his cap to Jen - ny Wren, Re - quest - ing to be heard.

1   'Twas on a merry time,
    When Jenny Wren was young,
  So neatly as she danced,
    And so sweetly as she sung;
  Robin Redbreast lost his heart,
    He was a gallant bird,
  He doffed his cap to Jenny Wren,
    Requesting to be heard.

2   My dearest Jenny Wren,
    If you will but be mine,
  You shall dine on cherry pie,
    And drink nice currant wine;
  I'll dress you like a goldfinch,
    Or like a peacock gay,
  So if you'll have me, Jenny dear,
    Let us appoint the day.

3   Jenny blushed behind her fan
    And thus declared her mind:
  So let it be tomorrow, Rob,
    I'll take your offer kind;
  Cherry pie is very good,
    And so is currant wine;
  But I will wear my plain brown dress,
    And never dress too fine.

4   Robin Redbreast got up early,
    All at the break of day,
  He flew to Jenny Wren's house
    And sang a roundelay;
  He sang of Robin Redbreast,
    And pretty Jenny Wren,
  And when he came unto the end,
    He then began again.

DAME, GET UP AND BAKE
YOUR PIES

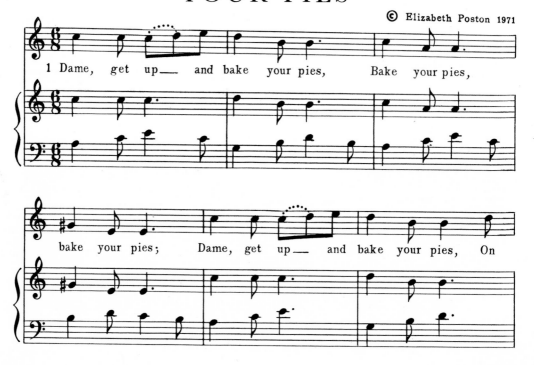

1 Dame, get up__ and bake your pies, Bake your pies, bake your pies; Dame, get up__ and bake your pies, On

Christ - mas day in the morn - ing.

1 Dame, get up and bake your pies,
   Bake your pies, bake your pies;
   Dame, get up and bake your pies,
   On Christmas day in the morning.

2 Dame, what makes your maidens lie,
   Maidens lie, maidens lie;
   Dame, what makes your maidens lie,
   On Christmas day in the morning?

3 Dame, what makes your ducks to die,
   Ducks to die, ducks to die;
   Dame, what makes your ducks to die,
   On Christmas day in the morning?

4 Their wings are cut and they cannot fly,
   Cannot fly, cannot fly;
   Their wings are cut and they cannot fly,
   On Christmas day in the morning.

THE CARRION CROW

© Elizabeth Poston 1971

1 A car - rion crow sat on an oak,

Der - ry der-ry der - ry, dec - co; A car - rion crow sat

on an oak, Watch-ing a tai - lor shape his cloak.

Heigh ho! the car-rion crow, Der-ry der-ry der - ry, dec - co.

1 A carrion crow sat on an oak,
   Derry derry derry, decco;
A carrion crow sat on an oak,
Watching a tailor shape his cloak.
   Heigh ho! the carrion crow,
   Derry derry derry, decco.

2 O wife, bring me my old bent bow,
   Derry derry derry, decco;
O wife, bring me my old bent bow,
That I may shoot yon carrion crow.
   Heigh ho! the carrion crow,
   Derry derry derry, decco.

3 The tailor shot and missed his mark,
   Derry derry derry, decco;
The tailor shot and missed his mark,
And shot his old sow through the heart.
   Heigh ho! the carrion crow,
   Derry derry derry, decco.

4 O wife, bring brandy in a spoon,
   Derry derry derry, decco;
O wife, bring brandy in a spoon,
For our old sow is in a swoon,
   Heigh ho! the carrion crow,
   Derry derry derry, decco.

ST PAUL'S STEEPLE

Up - on Paul's stee - ple stands a tree As
full of ap - ples as may be; The lit - tle boys of
Lon - don town They run with hooks to pull them down; And
then they run from hedge to hedge Un -

til they come to Lon - don Bridge.

Upon Paul's steeple stands a tree
As full of apples as may be;
The little boys of London town
They run with hooks to pull them down;
And then they run from hedge to hedge
Until they come to London Bridge.

MARIA LAVAVA
MARY WASHED LINEN

© Elizabeth Poston 1971
Words and tune coll. E.P.

Ma - ri - a la - va - va, Giu - sep - pe ten - de - va, Il bam-
While Ma - ry washed li - nen, Jo - seph spread it dry - ing, The

bi - no pian - ge - va Dal son - no che a - ve - va. Stai
ba - by was slee - py And sore - ly was cry - ing. O

zit - to, mio fi-glio, Ch'a - des - so ti pi-glio, Ti
hush you, my ba - by, For now I will tend you, I'll

pi - glio e ti fa - scio La nan - na ti fo, Ti
take you and I'll rock you And sing lul - la - by, I'll

pi - glio e ti fa - scio La nan - na ti fo.
take you and I'll rock you And sing___ lul - la - by.

Maria lavava,	While Mary washed linen,
Giuseppe tendeva,	Joseph spread it drying,
Il bambino piangeva	The baby was sleepy
Dal sonno che aveva.	And sorely was crying.
Stai zitto, mio figlio,	O hush you, my baby,
Ch'adesso ti piglio,	For now I will tend you,
Ti piglio e ti fascio	I'll take you and I'll rock you
La nanna ti fo,	And sing lullaby,
Ti piglio e ti fascio	I'll take you and I'll rock you
La nanna ti fo.	And sing lullaby.

PITTY PATTY POLT

© Elizabeth Poston 1971
Words and tune coll. E.P.

Pit - ty pat - ty polt, Shoe the wild__ colt,

Here a nail, and there a nail, Pit - ty pat - ty polt.

Pitty patty polt,
Shoe the wild colt,
Here a nail, and there a nail,
Pitty patty polt.

LONDON BRIDGE

1 Lon - don Bridge is bro - ken down,

Dance o - ver my la - dy lea; Lon - don Bridge is

bro - ken down, *With a gay* la - dy.

1 London Bridge is broken down,
   Dance over my lady lea;
London Bridge is broken down,
   With a gay lady.

2 How shall we build it up again?
   Dance over my lady lea;
How shall we build it up again?
   With a gay lady.

3 Build it up with silver and gold,
   Dance over my lady lea;
Build it up with silver and gold,
   With my gay lady.

4 Silver and gold will be stole away,
   Dance over my lady lea;
Silver and gold will be stole away,
   With a gay lady.

5 Build it up with iron and steel,
   Dance over my lady lea;
Build it up with iron and steel,
   With a gay lady.

6 Iron and steel will bend and bow,
   Dance over my lady lea;
Iron and steel will bend and bow,
   With a gay lady.

7 Build it up with wood and clay,
   Dance over my lady lea;
Build it up with wood and clay,
   With a gay lady.

8 Wood and clay will wash away,
   Dance over my lady lea;
Wood and clay will wash away,
   With a gay lady.

9 Build it up with stone so strong,
   Dance over my lady lea;
Huzza! 'twill last for ages long.
   With a gay lady.

PAT-A-CAKE

Pat-a-cake, pat-a-cake, ba-ker's man, Bake me a cake as fast as you can; Pat it and prick it, and mark it with B, Put it in the o-ven for ba-by and me, For ba-by and me, for

ba - by and me, Put it in the o - ven for ba - by and me.

Pat-a-cake, pat-a-cake, baker's man,
Bake me a cake as fast as you can;
Pat it and prick it, and mark it with B,
Put it in the oven for baby and me.

THE SCARECROW

O all you lit - tle black - ey tops, Pray don't you eat my fa - ther's crops, While I lie down and take a nap. *Shoo -*

a _____ O! _____ Shoo - a _____ O! _____

O all you little blackey tops,
Pray don't you eat my father's crops,
While I lie down and take a nap.
    Shoo-a O!
    Shoo-a O!

THE OLD WOMAN
TOSSED UP IN A BLANKET

There was an old wo-man tossed up in a blan - ket,

Sev - en - teen times as high as the moon; Where she was

go - ing I could - n't but ask it, For in her hand she

car-ried a broom. Old wo-man, old wo-man, old wo-man, quoth
I, O where are you go-ing to, up— so high? To sweep the
cob-webs off— the sky! May I— go with you? Aye, by and by.

There was an old woman tossed up in a blanket,
Seventeen times as high as the moon;
Where she was going I couldn't but ask it,
For in her hand she carried a broom.
Old woman, old woman, old woman, quoth I,
O where are you going to, up so high?
To sweep the cobwebs off the sky!
May I go with you?
Aye, by and by.

NEW YEAR'S DAY
IN THE MORNING

1 I saw three ships come sail - ing by,

Sail - ing by, sail - ing by, I saw three ships come

sail - ing by On New Year's Day in the morn - ing.

I saw three ships come sailing by,
   Sailing by, sailing by,
I saw three ships come sailing by
   On New Year's Day in the morning.

And what do you think was in them then,
   In them then, in them then,
And what do you think was in them then?
   On New Year's Day in the morning.

3 Three pretty girls were in them then,
   In them then, in them then,
Three pretty girls were in them then
   On New Year's Day in the morning.

4 And one could whistle, and one could sing,
   And one could play on the violin;
Such joy was there at my wedding
   On New Year's Day in the morning.

DIN, DON
DING DONG, DING DANG DONG

1 Din, don, din, don, dan, cam-pa-ni-tas__ so-na-
1 Ding, dong, ding, dang, dong, lit-tle bells are__ ring-ing

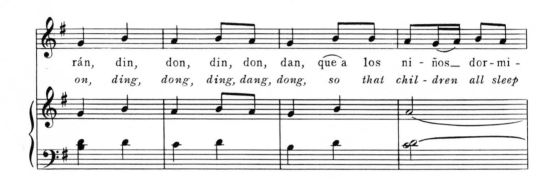

rán, din, don, din, don, dan, que a los ni-ños__ dor-mi-
on, ding, dong, ding, dang, dong, so that chil-dren all sleep

rán. Duer-me tran-qui-lo, mi bien, duér-me-te, que yo tu
on. Sleep and rest qui-et, my love, go to sleep, that safe and

sue-ño fe-liz guar-da-ré. Din, don, din, don,
hap-py your rest I may keep. Ding, dong, ding, dang,

dan, cam-pa-ni-tas__ so-na - rán. _____

dong, lit-tle bells are__ ring-ing on. _____

1 Din, don, din, don, dan,
campanitas sonarán,
din, don, din, don, dan,
que a los niños dormirán.
Duerme tranquilo,
mi bien, duérmete,
que yo tu sueño
feliz guardaré.
Din, don, din, don, dan,
campanitas sonarán.

1 Ding, dong, ding, dang, dong,
little bells are ringing on,
ding, dong, ding, dang, dong,
so that children all sleep on.
Sleep and rest quiet,
my love, go to sleep,
that safe and happy
your rest I may keep.
Ding, dong, ding, dang, dong,
little bells are ringing on.

2 Din, don, din, don, dan,
las estrellas brillarán,
din, don, din, don, dan,
y a los niños velarán.
Cierra los ojos
y duérmete ya,
porque la noche
muy pronto vendrá.
Din, don, din, don, dan,
las estrellas brillarán.

2 Ding, dong, ding, dang, dong,
all the stars are shining on,
ding, dong, ding, dang, dong,
over children they watch on.
Close now your eyelids
and go to sleep soon,
for it is time
for the night to draw on.
Ding, dong, ding, dang, dong,
all the stars are shining on.

3 Din, don, din, don, dan,
angelitos bajarán,
din, don, din, don, dan,
que a los niños besarán.
Duerme y sonríe
que yo estoy aquí,
niño querido,
velando por ti.
Din, don, din, don, dan,
angelitos bajarán.

3 Ding, dong, ding, dang, dong,
little angels will come down,
ding, dong, ding, dang, dong,
they'll kiss children as their own.
Sleep child and smile now
your mother's close by,
watching and singing
her dear lullabye.
Ding, dong, ding, dang, dong,
little angels will come down.

HICKORY, DICKORY, DOCK

Hick - o - ry, dick - o - ry, dock, _____ The mouse ran up _____ the clock. _____ The clock struck one, The mouse ran down, Hick - o - ry, dick - o - ry, dock. _____

Hickory, dickory, dock,
The mouse ran up the clock.
The clock struck one,
The mouse ran down,
Hickory, dickory, dock.

HUMPTY DUMPTY

Hump — ty Dump — ty sat on a wall,

Hump — ty Dump — ty had a great fall;

All the king's hor - ses And all the king's men

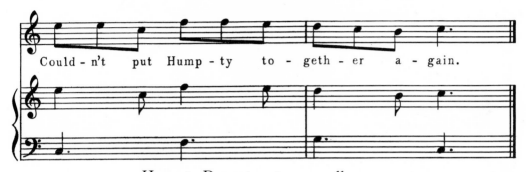

Could - n't put Hump - ty to - geth - er a - gain.

Humpty Dumpty sat on a wall,
Humpty Dumpty had a great fall;
   All the king's horses
   And all the king's men
Couldn't put Humpty together again.

THE OLD GREY GOOSE

1 Go tell Aunt Rho - dy,

Go tell Aunt Rho - dy, Go tell Aunt

Rho - dy The old grey goose is dead.

1   Go tell Aunt Rhody,
Go tell Aunt Rhody,
Go tell Aunt Rhody
The old grey goose is dead.

2   The one she's been savin',
The one she's been savin',
The one she's been savin'
To make a feather bed.

3   She died on the millpond,   (*three times*)
Standing on her head.

4   The goslin's are cryin',   (*three times*)
Because their mother's dead.

LITTLE JACK HORNER

© Elizabeth Poston 1971

Lit - tle Jack Hor - ner Sat in the cor - ner,

Eat - ing a Christ - mas pie; —————— He

put in his thumb, And pulled out a plum, And

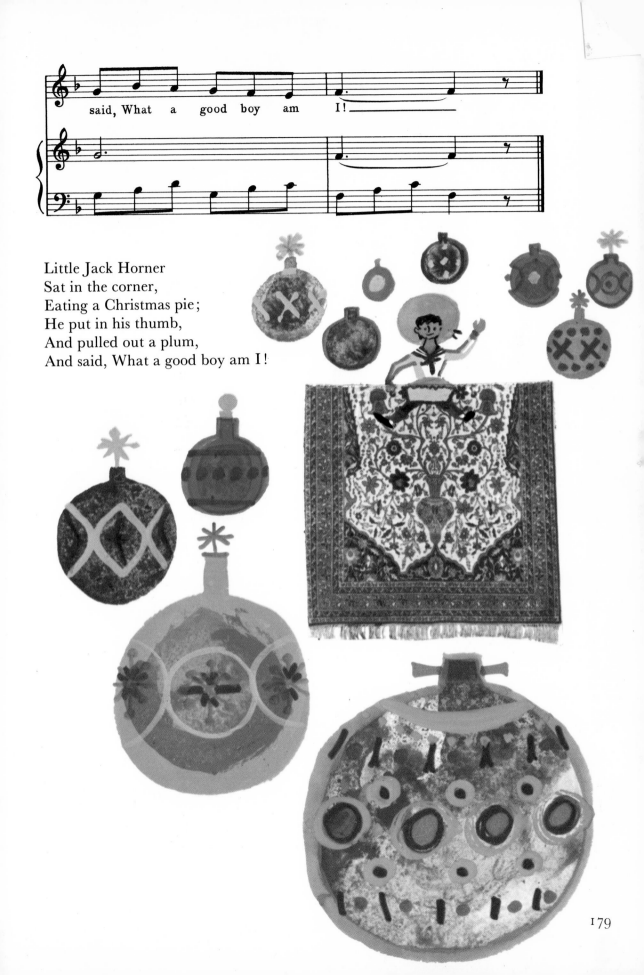

said, What a good boy am I! _____

Little Jack Horner
Sat in the corner,
Eating a Christmas pie;
He put in his thumb,
And pulled out a plum,
And said, What a good boy am I!

FRERE JACQUES
BROTHER JAMES

Frè - re Jac - ques, Frè - re Jac - ques, Dor - mez - vous?
Bro - ther James, O Bro - ther James, Are you a - sleep?

Dor - mez - vous? Son - nez les ma - ti - nes,
You a - sleep? Ring the bell for ma - tins,

Son-nez les ma-ti-nes, Din, dan, don, Din, dan, don.
Ring the bell for ma-tins, Ding, dang, dong, Ding, dang, dong.

Frère Jacques,
Frère Jacques,
Dormez-vous?
Dormez-vous?
Sonnez les matines,
Sonnez les matines,
　Din, dan, don,
　Din, dan, don.

Brother James,
O Brother James,
Are you asleep?
You asleep?
Ring the bell for matins,
Ring the bell for matins,
　Ding, dang, dong,
　Ding, dang, dong.

INDEX OF FIRST LINES
AND
INDEX OF TITLES

INDEX OF FIRST LINES

INDEX OF TITLES

ABOUT THE AUTHOR

Elizabeth Poston lives in Hertfordshire, England, where she was born. "My earliest recollection is of being sung to sleep in the night with a nursery rhyme," she says. She was educated privately, at the Royal Academy of Music, and in Europe. During her poststudent years she was once locked up with a goat in a prison cell in southern Europe, but was released when she proved to be carrying not code but folk songs. Returning to England, she joined the BBC's staff. She resigned later to pursue her own work, but acted as adviser, producer, and composer at the inception of the BBC's famed Third Programme. She has traveled widely, distinguishing herself in almost all fields of music, and has covered unusually wide ground creatively in both words and music in the concert hall, theater, church, films, radio, television, and records, as well as in the field of music education. Of *The Baby's Song Book* she says, "it reflects particularly my concern for the standard of all publications both visually and in context. . . . I hold as of prime importance the need to preserve the basic essence, whether by picture or in words and music, rhyme and folk song, of anything of these published for children: that it be true to itself within its element."

ABOUT THE ARTIST

William Stobbs has had an equally distinguished career as artist, illustrator, and educator. He shares Elizabeth Poston's meticulousness in research and her pleasure in introducing traditional beauty to children. He has illustrated many books for young people and has been awarded the Kate Greenaway Medal for his work. Principal of the Maidstone College of Art in Kent, Mr. Stobbs lives with his wife, who is also an artist, and their children in a lovely old half-timbered house not far from the college.